Dear Mommy's Boss

A Kid's Perspective of the Corporate Workplace

SYDNEY W. JOSHUA

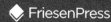 FriesenPress

Suite 300 - 990 Fort St
Victoria, BC, V8V 3K2
Canada

www.friesenpress.com

ISBN
978-1-5255-8712-2 (Hardcover)
978-1-5255-8713-9 (Paperback)
978-1-5255-8714-6 (eBook)

1. FICTION, SATIRE

Distributed to the trade by The Ingram Book Company

For the bosses who recognize that people matter and that some of the so-called "urgent" memos can wait until morning. The children thank you.

Dear Mommy's Boss,

Thank you for letting Mommy work part time when I was in her tummy. She was so nauseous that she couldn't even work right. You didn't seem bothered when she wore out a path to the bathroom from her office and was so nauseous that she told the paying clients that they could take their time paying because it wasn't a rush (sorry about that). In hindsight, she wasn't thinking straight because it was hard to work the right way, while crouched over the garbage can with ginger tea on the side. Anyway, Mommy still doesn't know how she got a raise that year because she often put your work on the back burner when she needed a quick nap. After all, carrying me around was a job in and of itself. She'll never forget how understanding you were.

Ellis

P. S. I know all of this because I was in her tummy, and I heard her telling people with bad bosses that you weren't bad (because you didn't get bent out of shape when she was nauseous. . . not actually working the real, right, regular way).

Dear Mommy's Boss,

Thank you for letting Mommy stay home with me until I was six months old. I didn't even need to go to daycare when I was born because you let her stay home with me. Mommy felt so appreciated because she still got her full pay and bonus even though she wasn't working as good as she usually worked. Apparently, you had a deal to send work home, but you acted like you forgot about that deal because you hardly ever sent work home. You just wanted her to spend time with me and not do much work. She said this made sense because in the past you overworked her anyway, so basically it was a wash. In fact, Dad blames you for my clinginess because if you sent work home then I wouldn't be so clingy because I wouldn't have been carried around as much. Lucky me ... I got to be carried around, having all of my unreasonable demands met non-stop for six straight months. I had the time of my life! Oh, how I miss those days . . .

Kendall

Dear Mommy's Boss,

Thank you for letting Mommy leave the office early sometimes, so she could see the opening solos at my school concerts. She was never late. Not even once. Mommy got to see how great I looked on the stage (people told me I looked great, which is how I know). Everybody clapped for me when I played. I got a standing ovation and everything. I almost played as good as Stevie Wonder and Billy Joel (except Stevie Wonder and Billy Joel are a little bit better).

Brandon

Dear Mommy's Boss,

Thank you for telling Mommy that she shouldn't bring me to the office on the weekends to do overtime (because it stinks for a kid to have to do overtime on the weekend). It was a good idea for you to give us (I mean *her*) a computer at home, so she could do work after I went to sleep or while I was outside riding my bike. The best part was pretending to my friends that the fancy computer was mine, even though it wasn't. Mommy got a lot of work done on the computer even though I accidently broke some of the keys here and there. I mean, it didn't matter that much about the broken keys because the computer was at home, so you didn't actually have to see the damage. Anyway, broken keys and all, she managed.

Catherine

Dear Mommy's Boss,

Thank you for letting Mommy take a two-hour lunch break, so she could meet my teacher to talk about me. They wanted to talk about how good I'm doing in school and everything. Mommy said she and Mrs. Williams didn't even have to rush talking about how smart I am because Mommy was in no rush to go back to the office. She told Mrs. Williams that she didn't have to rush because your work wasn't that important. I mean, your work was probably a little bit important, but it was definitely not as important as my parent-teacher conference, so they had a lot of time to chitchat on company time (because your work wasn't really urgent, even though you thought it was).

Dillon

Dear Mommy's Boss,

Thank you for letting Mommy leave work at 5:20 instead of 5:30 every day. She said that the ten-minute lead let her catch the 5:45 train home so that I didn't have to be the last one picked up from daycare. Let me tell you about that. Being the last one picked up stinks because the daycare people leave you at the door with your bag and the lights are almost all out while you're waiting to be picked up. I know this because the *one* day that Daddy picked me up, I was last. If you weren't Mommy's boss, I would be sitting in the dark *every day* (not just on the days Daddy picked me up).

Brad

Dear Mommy's Boss,

Thank you for giving Mommy a gift certificate for Burlington Coat Factory for her birthday. I was tired of going there every two weeks to put money on layaway. Lucky for her (and me), you gave her that certificate, so she would not be cold all winter because at the rate she was going, she would not have picked up the coat until spring. You could have easily gone across the street and given her a gift card to Saks Fifth Avenue like you did for the other staff, but you went out of your way to go all the way downtown to Burlington. Mommy cried tears of joy. Now, you probably only did it so she wouldn't get sick from the cold and have to take time off from work (but we can overlook that because we're not petty). Just know that after your gift we only went back to that store one more time to finally pick up her coat. And that was that!

Erin

Dear Mommy's Boss,

Thank you for letting Mommy use the company card to take Daddy out for his birthday dinner. We would have been embarrassed because the waitress said Mommy's credit card was broken, so she used yours instead. It's a good thing she used the company credit card because then Daddy would have had to wash dishes. I don't know what washing dishes means, but I hear that is what people sometimes have to do when their credit cards are broken in restaurants. Dad was so relieved you were Mommy's boss and that you didn't mind that she used the company credit card willy nilly once in a while. Mom claims that she never used the company card willy nilly because she always paid it back, but Dad called it willy nilly—whatever willy nilly is.

Joy

Dear Mommy's Boss,

Thank you for telling Mommy not to call you while we were on vacation at Disneyworld (and thank you for not calling her). Because if you had called and interrupted a photo shoot with Mickey, I would not have been happy (and neither would Mickey because Mickey has a long line, and you would have held up the line if you called). Oh, and Mommy says the reason she always makes sure to buy you a gift on our vacations is because she says that you give her a gift every day. I don't know what that means, but it must mean something good.

Ilene

Dear Mommy's Boss,

Thank you for not looking at Mommy like she was from Jupiter when she said she had to leave work early to take Quincy to the vet. Even though you only have fish (which are not real pets), you knew that Mommy had to get Quincy to the vet due to that little (self-inflicted) emergency he got himself into. Which reminds me, somebody should tell dogs to *only* eat what's in their bowl. Anyway, Quincy is grateful that you are Mommy's boss, and my family is grateful that you know that dogs are real pets, and they sometimes need to go to the vet . . . even though it's not always in the plans.

Mary

Dear Mommy's Boss,

Did I ever thank you for those scrumptious dinners you used to order on the nights you guys worked late? The chicken fingers, fish and chips, and sliders were such a great treat from the same old regular dinners we ate at home. Mom tolerated working late sometimes because she knew you would order good dinners for all the workers (somehow, I was always a part of the order). She said ordering extra food for me wasn't a big deal because you wouldn't notice it being that you weren't the one picking up the food from the delivery guy in the lobby. Plus, by the time that bill came in nobody would be thinking about a few extra treats on my behalf. I mean, let's face it, Mom kind of had to order the fish and chips . . . and sliders . . . and chicken fingers . . . and brownies . . . and chocolate chip cookies for me because otherwise what would I eat all week? Lets face it, she can't cook for me if she's working late for you. Thank goodness you always ordered from the good restaurants and not the bad ones.

Valerie

Dear Mommy's Boss,

Now that I'm a little older, I don't get to come into the office as much because I have all of these Little League games after school. I have to say I'm a little surprised you haven't asked about me. Don't you miss the days when the after-school center would close for vacation, and I would be at the office all day? Mom was so grateful that she could bring me to work sometimes on my days off from school. You still kept a great spirit when you arrived at the office and saw me spinning around on your rolling chair one day. I spun so fast I almost fell off. Everyone was laughing. Actually, were you laughing? Now that I think about it, I don't think you were actually laughing.

Donovan

Dear Mommy's Boss,

I just wanted to give you an update and tell you that because of you I made the most Girl Scout cookie sales! Mom said you didn't notice that she was walking around the office for two weeks with the order form. Dad said it would be easier if Mom just left the order form in her office, and people could come to her, but she said that wasn't the best idea because then you would think she wasn't working if she had all these people congregating (that means hanging around) in her office ordering cookies all day. So, instead, she walked around all day to all of the floors (not working), so that you wouldn't notice that she wasn't actually working.

Chelsea

Dear Mommy's Boss,

How do you like your new personal refrigerator that we got you for your birthday? Mom decided that you needed a bigger personal refrigerator in your office because she didn't have enough room for her stuff. You deserve it. Enjoy!

Felicia

Dear Mommy's Boss,

Have you ever considered inviting the kids to that fancy staff appreciation party that you have every year? You always say we are one big family, but kids aren't invited. The pictures always show the workers looking happy and having fun. They try out all of the fancy foods, and the waiters and waitresses are all dressed up in their fancy black tuxedos and white gloves. Mom says you always pick fancy restaurants to show your appreciation for the staff, but you and I both know it's a little too fancy for the staff. Some of them only go out to fancy places and get dressed up like that once a year, so they don't even know how to act like their normal selves when they go to high-society places like that. You should really consider inviting the kids. We can join in to make it a more realistic party. After all, a party isn't a party unless somebody spills something.

Christopher

Dear Mommy's Boss,

Now that I'm getting older, it's time to look back and reflect on the good old days and fun times that were had in the company playroom. The bouncy seat and old-fashioned building blocks were my favorite things to play with when Mom left me there for God knows how long because she couldn't watch me while she was in a meeting with you and other important people. Those were fun times, but because we are family, I just want to mention that it wouldn't kill you to put more noisy toys in the playroom. Your toys were too quiet. The classic wooden blocks with the letters on them are great and everything, but you should consider upgrading to the blocks that have the loud beads inside. That way the entire office can hear us, and it will save people from poking their head in to check on the kids every 2 minutes. They'll be able to hear us if there were noisy toys! Well, that's the only advice I have for you right now before I head off to kindergarten since, for the most part, your playroom was actually pretty good.

Kristi

Dear Mommy's Boss,
(This is an emergency follow-up letter!)

Kindergarten is cool, but it's busy, so I'm going to keep this short. Forget the noisy blocks that I suggested earlier. The school doesn't have them either because they claim they are very expensive and noisy. I didn't know they were expensive, so scratch that idea because if you spend money on those expensive blocks for the company playroom, you may not be able to give us (I mean Mom) the usual bonus at the end of the year. Not having a bonus would be an absolute disaster because no holiday bonus probably means no gifts under the Christmas tree for me. Quite frankly, that just doesn't add up.

Kristi

Dear Mommy's Boss,

You're such a good guy sending Mommy home in the Lincoln Town Car when she was in pain with the wisdom tooth. She was able to stretch out and rest in the back instead of taking the crowded train home. Our neighbors were going "Ooooh, aaahhh" when they saw the luxury company car pull up to the house. As a matter of fact, the more I think about it, the more I realize the wisdom tooth misery was a blessing in disguise. After that saga Mommy realized there was so much room in the company car that it would be a good idea to use it for personal stuff too, like going to the airport when our family takes a vacation. It's also great for holiday shopping. Everything fits in that spacious trunk, so we can shop till we drop! I don't know if you know about this arrangement, but it has been working well ever since the wisdom tooth fiasco. Since then, the drivers pencil us in for our annual vacation and holiday shopping trips. With the tips Mom gives them, they actually look forward to chauffeuring us around. And, of course, you don't mind because you're such a good boss.

Darren

Dear Mommy's Boss,

You're so great. Mommy got all the way to the transfer point at the train station and could not remember if she turned off the iron. That was very scary and not typical Mommy behavior. It was very unsettling. So, she crossed the train platform and took another one home. Mom was so mad at herself because that meant she'd be late for work. But when she called to explain the situation to you, all you said was, "No worries. We hope the house is still standing when you get there."

And that was that. No song and no dance.

Michael

Dear Mommy's Boss,

It's the simple things that go a long way for Mommy's who have latchkey kids. Like the way I called Mommy at the office every day at 3:15 p.m. to let her know I was off the school bus. The conversation always lasted longer than two minutes because I always forgot to wait to make that call until I actually got into the house. I'm sorry that many of your important incoming calls got sent to voicemail around that time, but eventually, important clients learned to call at better times. They learned that 3:15 meant they got the voicemail because Mommy was making sure I got into the house safely. What a great boss you were because you never noticed that calls from paying clients went to voicemail at that time. Just know it was for the greater good.

Ava

Dear Mommy's Boss,

The staff summer cookout in the park is one of the best events of the entire summer. It's great that you have the wherewithal to invite the kids to that since we are still not invited to the holiday party (I'm not sure how you keep forgetting to invite us to that). Anyway, the company is clever in planning the party on a day that we don't have camp, like July 4th or a Saturday or Sunday. That's all well and good, but the parks are pretty crowded on those days. Maybe you should consider a cozier place... like your house. Your backyard is a good idea so that little kids like me don't get lost in the massive park, and adults can relax and not have to watch us. I heard you have a pool, a barbeque grill, and a trampoline! Let's give this some thought. What else do you have?

Vinny

To My Corporate Bosses,

Thank you for being consistent, reliable, and grounded in reality. You created an environment where efficiency, production, and high-quality work was always the outcome **because you understood and cared about the real people behind the work.**

Thank you for the wonderful years.

SWJ

About the Author

Sydney W. Joshua is in the midst of her second career as a professional educator while simultaneously pursuing her interest in writing. In addition to teaching, she is the founder of Peak Educational Systems, an education consulting business. Although her first career in the legal industry is not known for having "good bosses," Sydney had the good fortune of working for bosses who she describes as "real." They deserve public praise and are the inspiration for this book.

In addition to writing, Sydney can be found at the yoga studio, the dog park, or frolicking the beautiful beaches of Long Island.

Dedication

This book is dedicated to the memory of Robert M. Peak, Esq. I also want to acknowledge Michael D. Schiano, Esq. and my Reboul, MacMurray, Hewitt, Maynard & Kristol family. Finally, to Edward L. Birnbaum, Esq., who saw something special in me and hired me to work at a big Wall Street firm before the ink was even dry on my college degree.

A great big THANK YOU for trusting the members of our team to get the job done ... *even if it wasn't always during regular work hours.*

Printed in the USA
CPSIA information can be obtained
at www.ICGtesting.com
CBHW070804040224
4015CB00032BB/1900

9 781525 587139